Am I Even a Bee?

Muth  Lindauer

Am I Even a Bee?

story by Felicity Muth

illustrations by Alexa Lindauer

BAOBAB PRESS

First Edition

22 23 24   10 9 8 7 6 5 4 3 2
ISBN-13: 978-1-956097-40-1
ISBN-10: 1-956097-40-0
Library of Congress Control Number: 2021949829

Baobab Press
121 California Avenue
Reno, Nevada
www.baobabpress.com

Made in Korea

MIX
Paper | Supporting
responsible forestry
FSC® C102582
FSC
www.fsc.org

In a meadow, at the end of last spring, Osmia's mother laid an egg in a bed of pollen. She tucked Osmia in and left her a note for when she was grown.

A year later, all grown up, Osmia still lived in the same meadow, visiting flowers every day to collect nectar and pollen.

She loved to buzz through the flowers.
Nectar from the blue ones was her favorite.

But lately, Osmia had been feeling uneasy.

Everywhere she looked, she saw bees, and not just in her meadow.

Bees in magazines, bees on t-shirts, and even children wearing bee costumes. What made Osmia feel troubled was that those bees all looked the same.

What's more, even some of the flies, moths, and beetles in the meadow looked like those bees.

But Osmia did not.

Those bees were round . . .

Those bees were fluffy . . .

Those bees were yellow and black . . .

. . . Osmia was slender.

. . . her hair was patchy.

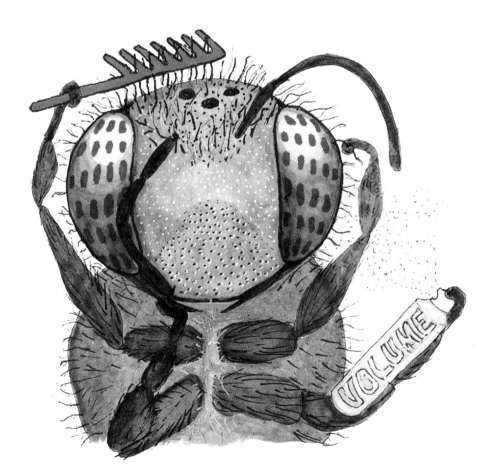

. . . she was bluey-green.

Those bees were social, always hanging out in a group.

Osmia lived alone in a hole.

Osmia had an idea. If flies and moths could pass as bees, maybe she could too. If she could just look more like them, then she would fit in. She painted herself with yellow stripes and stuck on some fluff she found in an old bird's nest.

It didn't work.

Suddenly, Osmia was startled by a swarm of bees buzzing by her home.

"Pardon me!"

"Excuse me!"

"Outta the way!" the honey bees said.

"So much for some quiet time to think," sighed Osmia.

Osmia flew around her meadow to sort her thoughts, landing on a flower. Her mother's note said she was a bee, but Osmia wasn't so sure. She began to wonder if she was even a bee at all.

"Maybe a drink of nectar will cheer me up," thought Osmia, but looking for her favorite blue flower, she flew straight into a big, black shape.

"So sorry! Are you okay, little bee?"

The black shape could speak!

"Name's Xylocopa. My friends call me Xyla."

The black shape also had a name.

"I'm Osmia, and I'm not okay."

"Whatever do you mean?" asked Xyla.

"You called me a bee, and I'm not sure if that is true. I don't look like what a bee is supposed to look like—yellow and black and fluffy and round."

"Things aren't always as they seem," said Xyla. "Look at me, do I have yellow and black stripes?"

"No," said Osmia.

"Am I fluffy?"

"No," said Osmia.

"Well, there you go. People call me a carpenter bee, but what I build doesn't always come out as planned," said Xyla.

"I <u>AM</u> a bee though, and proud of it," said Xyla. "If you look closer, you'll notice we have some things in common. Can you see what is the same?"

Osmia looked hard, searching for what was the same. At first, they seemed so different. Xyla was large and black, while she was small with a bright sheen that moved from green to blue. Osmia looked harder still, and then . . .

"Yes!" said Osmia, "we both have two big eyes on the sides of our heads, and three small eyes on the top of our heads!"

"That's right," said Xyla. "You may not be as different as you think."

"You visit flowers every day, but have you ever talked to your neighbors?" asked Xyla. "I think it's time you met some of the other bees in our meadow."

Osmia and Xyla flew to the edge of the meadow where some cows stood munching grass.

Osmia and Xyla landed on a cow where a small bee was holding a drop of liquid.

"What is that?" asked Osmia

"Sweat," said the bee.

"Sweat?!" exclaimed Osmia. "Does it taste good?"

"Oh yes," said the bee, "I love the stuff. That's why they call me the sweat bee. But I don't just like sweat, I also like tears, like the ones from this cow. Yum! Try some!"

"We've actually got to get going," said Osmia.

"She didn't seem like me," said Osmia. "I don't drink sweat."

"She was different in some ways," said Xyla, "but did you see what was the same?"

Osmia thought. "Yes! She has four wings, just like you and me!"

"Right again," said Xyla.

"What's going on over there?" asked Osmia.

"That's Nomada," said Xyla. "She's a cuckoo bee."

"I didn't realize bees could be red!" said Osmia. "Wow, bees come in all the colors of the rainbow! I hope you don't mind me asking, Nomada, but why aren't you fluffy?"

"Fluff is useful when you want to be covered in pollen to take home to feed to your babies. That's not my style though—I don't collect pollen. Instead, I leave my eggs in my friend's nest, and she takes care of them."

Osmia and Xyla moved on through the grass. "I'm not sure I trust Nomada," muttered Osmia.

"But did she have four wings, two eyes on the side of her head, and three eyes on top?" asked Xyla.

"You're right!" exclaimed Osmia. "I can trust that she's a bee."

"Shhh, be careful not to wake that digger bee," said Xyla. "He's taking a nap."

"Why is he called a digger bee?" Osmia whispered.

"Look over there," said Xyla.

Osmia looked and saw many bees, furiously digging.

"They live in holes, just like me!" she said.

Osmia looked across her meadow, and for the first time, she didn't just see flowers. Instead, she saw bees everywhere. Bees of many colors. Bees of many sizes. All different, but all bees.

"Now I see", said Osmia "There are many ways to be a bee."

Am I striped and fluffy,
like other bees you've seen?
Not I, in fact I'm painted
with a bright metallic sheen.

I glint, I gleam, I dazzle
with colors just for me.
One thing I know for certain,
I am certainly a bee.

Do I live with others
in a busy, noisy hive?
No, I am happy in my hole,
on my own I really thrive.

Although I seem quite different
from other bees you see,
one thing I know for certain,
I am certainly a bee.

The sweat bee sips on others' tears
or sometimes sweat is best.
Nomada bees, like cuckoos,
Lay eggs in others' nests.

We all have four wings to fly
And five eyes with which to see,
That's how I know for certain,
I am certainly a bee.

So the honey bees can keep their dance,
And Xyla, her carpentry.
One thing I know for certain,
There's no one way to be a bee.

To my parents, for fostering my interest in insects from a young age. And to Martha and Herb for introducing me to the wonderful Reno community. - F.M.

To James, with love. - A.L.